This Walker book belongs to:

_____

_____

_____

With love to all the children and staff at Aspire Nursery - and most of
all to Vasilis. Thank you for the joy and inspiration.
- J.P

For Joe, I love you
- M.P.S

With thanks to Louise Jackson and Denise Johnstone-Burt

First published 2019 by Walker Books Ltd, 87 Vauxhall Walk, London SE11 5HJ
This edition published 2020

2 4 6 8 10 9 7 5 3 1

This book has been typeset in Filosofia

Printed in China

British Library Cataloguing in Publication Data: a catalogue record for this book is available from the British Library

ISBN 978-1-4063-9287-6

www.walker.co.uk

WALKER BOOKS
AND SUBSIDIARIES
LONDON • BOSTON • SYDNEY • AUCKLAND

THE BOY WHO LOVED EVERYONE

JANE PORTER   ILLUSTRATED BY MAISIE PARADISE SHEARRING

It was storytime. Everyone wriggled till they were ready to listen.

Dimitri was new at nursery. He leaned his head on Liam.

"I love you, Liam," he said.

Liam didn't know what to say, so he said nothing.

The teacher began the story.

It was about a dragon, a volcano

and a magic teapot.

At morning play, Dimitri found Sophie, Stella and Sue.

"I love you," he told them.

But they giggled and ran away.

So Dimitri went to the tree with the big heart-shaped leaves
and put his arms around it. "I love you, tree," he said.

The tree didn't reply.

Some ants marched past.

"Hello ants, I love you," said Dimitri,

but they kept on marching.

It was time for lunch. The food was good.
Berthe served a huge pile of pudding.

"I love you, Berthe," said Dimitri.

"You mean you love my custard!"
said Berthe.

That afternoon Dimitri said   the paintbrushes,

"I love you" to the class guinea pig,

love you
guinea pig

Big Andrew and Little Bea.

I love
you

But they joked or blushed or turned away,

and the guinea pig just burrowed

in the straw.

At home time, Dimitri told the teacher that he loved her.

"Dear Dimitri," she said, "I know you do. I'll see you tomorrow."

Dimitri walked with his mum past the bakery, through the park and over the canal. On a bench sat an old man who looked tired.

"I love you, old man," said Dimitri.

"Who are you calling old?" snapped the man, and he pulled his coat tighter around him.

After that Dimitri
was very quiet.

At bedtime he whispered,

"I love you, Mum."

"And I love you, Dimitri," she said.

"You're my best, best boy."

The next morning, Dimitri didn't want
to go to school.

"I told everyone I love them, and no one said it back."

Mum helped him put on his coat and wrapped him up warm.

"People have lots of different ways of showing how they feel," she said, as they walked towards the canal.

"When you tell people you love them, they feel it, even if you can't always see it," she explained. "Your love spreads out and grows in new places."

They saw the old man on the bench. He was opening a tin of tuna and feeding the stray cats breakfast.

"You see," said Mum, "he's saying 'I love you' to the cats."

In the park they saw Berthe on her way to school,

and she gave a big, big wave when she saw Dimitri.

"Look," said Mum, "she's saying it with her smile."

The playground tree with the heart-shaped leaves was filled with singing birds as Mum said goodbye. Beneath the branches, Sue, Stella and Sophie were feeding the birds. Dimitri looked at the tiny birds hopping with enjoyment and wished he could join the girls.

He stood on his own, feeling uncertain. But then Stella saw him.

"Come and help us, Dimitri," said the girls,
and they gave him a packet of birdseed.
One bird jumped onto his hand and
tickled his palm with its lightness.

Then Liam came over and gave Dimitri a hug.

"Hello my friend! Will you sit with me at storytime?" he said.

A warm feeling started to grow inside Dimitri.

When they got to storytime, EVERYONE wanted to sit with Dimitri.
They made quite a pile. The pile made the teacher laugh.

"You funny children," she said. "I do love you all."

This time the story was about a frog, a mountain, and a rabbit
who loved everyone.

Even the guinea pig enjoyed it.

Also by Jane Porter:

"A terrific read-aloud" – School Library Journal

PINK LION

Jane Porter

978-1-4063-6233-6